壮族神话传说少儿绘本

A Tale of Zhuang Brocade

一幅壮锦

编著：南宁市博物馆 / 广西霖创文化创意有限责任公司

广西美术出版社
GUANGXI FINE ARTS PUBLISHING HOUSE

图书在版编目（CIP）数据

一幅壮锦：中文、英文 / 南宁市博物馆，广西霖创文化
创意有限责任公司编著. —南宁：广西美术出版社，2020.12
（壮族神话传说少儿绘本）
ISBN 978-7-5494-2283-8

Ⅰ. ①一… Ⅱ. ①南… ②广… Ⅲ. ①儿童文学－图画故事－
中国－当代 Ⅳ. ①I287.8

中国版本图书馆CIP数据核字（2020）第234524号

一幅壮锦　壮族神话传说少儿绘本

YIFU ZHUANGJIN　　ZHUANGZU SHENHUA CHUANSHUO SHAO' ER HUIBEN

编　著：南宁市博物馆 / 广西霖创文化创意有限责任公司
主　编：张晓剑 / 覃　忠 / 周佳璐
编　委：刘德雨 / 吕虹霖 / 蓝　涛 / 潘昕昊 / 欧　文 / 彭　柯
　　　　梁　晨 / 咸　安 / 夏丽娜 / 黎琼泽 / 张沥仁 / 周　怡
绘　画：周佳璐 / 张云浩 / 王恩惠 / 冯　磊 / 李　琼
英文译者：姚小文
英文审校：[英] Judith Sovin

出　版　人：陈　明
终　　　审：邓　欣
策　划　编　辑：谭　宇
责　任　编　辑：黄　玲　谭　宇
装　帧　设　计：谭　宇
校　　　对：梁冬梅
审　　　读：肖丽新
出　版　发　行：广西美术出版社
地　　　址：广西南宁市望园路9号（邮编：530023）
网　　　址：www.gxfinearts.com
印　　　刷：广西壮族自治区地质印刷厂
版　次　印　次：2020年12月第1版第1次印刷
开　　　本：889mm×1194mm　1/16
印　　　张：2
字　　　数：10千字
书　　　号：ISBN 978-7-5494-2283-8
定　　　价：45.00元

很久很久以前，

在大山的脚下住着一位壮族妲布和她的三个儿子。

Once upon a time at the foot of a mountain,

there lived a Mother from the Zhuang ethnic group.

She lived with her three sons.

妲布织得一手好壮锦，

全家就靠妲布的手艺活来过日子。

The Mother was a skilled weaver of Zhuang brocade.

She supported her family by selling the brocades she wove.

一天，妲布去圩上卖锦的时候，看到一幅美丽的画，画上有高大的房屋、好看的花园、大片的田地，又有果园、菜园和鱼塘，还有成群的牛羊鸡鸭。妲布心里想：要是我能生活在这么一个村庄里就好了。

One day, the Mother went to the local market to sell her brocade. Suddenly, her eyes were drawn to a beautiful painting. The painting depicted a scene of spacious houses with beautiful gardens and large fields. There were orchards, vegetable gardens, fish ponds, cows, goats, ducks and chickens. The Mother sighed and thought to herself, "If only I could live in such a village."

妲布满心欢喜地买下了这幅画,
她决定把画上的美丽村庄织成一幅壮锦。

The Mother excitedly bought the painting and decided to
weave the beautiful village in the painting into a piece of Zhuang brocade.

妲布一回到家就开始不分昼夜地依照图画织起来。

松油灯把她的眼睛都熏坏了。

眼泪滴在锦上,

她就在眼泪上织起了小河、鱼塘;

眼血滴在锦上,

她就在眼血上织起了红红的太阳、鲜艳的花朵。

As soon as she arrived home,

the Mother set to work on her brocade version of the painting.

She worked day and night!

Her eyes were full of tears from the smoke of her pine oil lamps

and her tears dripped down onto the brocade. She wove rivers

and fish ponds in the tracks of her tears.

Then blood flowed from her tired eyes onto the brocade and over

the blood stains she wove the red sun and bright flowers.

就这样织呀织，织呀织，一共织了三年，

这幅大壮锦终于织好了！它可真美丽呀！

After three years of constant weaving,

the immense Zhuang brocade was finally completed.

It was magnificent!

一家人拿着壮锦来到院子里准备好好瞧瞧。

忽然，一阵大风刮过来，把壮锦卷出大门，

卷上天空，一直朝东方飞去。

妲布赶忙追了出去，摇摆着双手，仰着头喊叫。

啊呀！壮锦转眼就不见了。妲布伤心得昏倒在了大门外。

The family carried the brocade outside to the yard for a better look.
However, a gust of wind blew the brocade out of their hands and it flew up
into the sky towards the east.
The Mother chased it frantically, calling out and waving towards it.
Alas, the brocade soon flew out of sight.
The poor Mother fainted outside the gate.

妲布醒过来后，对大儿子说：

"你去东方寻回壮锦吧，

它是阿咪的命根啊！"

When she regained her consciousness,
the Mother asked her eldest son to go to
the east and retrieve the precious brocade.

大儿子走了一个月，到了一座大山隘口。

那里有一间石头房子，右边有一匹大石马，

门口坐着一个老奶奶。

The eldest son walked for a whole month before
he arrived at the mountain pass.
There was a stone house.
Standing on the right was a stone horse and
sitting in the doorway was an old granny.

老奶奶告诉大儿子是东方太阳山的仙女把壮锦借去做样子了。 "如果想要去找回来，你要骑上大石马，经过烈焰熊熊的火山和漂浮着冰块的大海，最后才能到达太阳山。如果不能坚持到底，你就会丧命。"

The granny told him that it was the fairies who lived on the Sun Mountain in the east that had borrowed his mother's precious Zhuang brocade.

They wanted it as an example of excellence.

"If you want to get it back, you will have to ride the big stone horse to climb the fire mountain that rages with ferocious flames. Then you will have to cross the ocean that is full of floating icy rocks. This is the only way you can reach the Sun Mountain. You will need to persevere or you will perish."

大儿子听完，吓得脸都青了，

老奶奶劝他不要去了，还送了他一盒金子。

大儿子拿了金子，跑到大城市享乐去了。

The eldest son was so terrified by these trials that he turned pale with fear. The granny found that he was easily persuaded to forget his task. She offered him a box of gold which he accepted and took to spend on himself in the big city.

妲布病倒在床上，不见大儿子回来，

又让二儿子去寻找。

和哥哥一样，二儿子也是个贪生怕死的人，

他也拿了老奶奶的金子，到大城市享乐去了。

The poor Mother lay bedridden with grief.
when the eldest son did not return,
she asked the middle son to go in search of
her Zhuang brocade.
Unfortunately, the middle son was also
a terrible coward like his elder brother.
He too took the gold and enjoyed himself
in the big city.

妲布病得更加严重了，眼睛都哭瞎了。

看到妈妈受苦，小儿子决心去把壮锦找回来。

The mother became more and more sickly and eventually
she became blind from shedding so many tears.
After witnessing his mother's suffering,
the youngest son was determined to find the brocade
and bring it back.

小儿子来到大山隘口，也见到了老奶奶。

他并没有害怕退缩，

也没有像两个哥哥那样拿了金子去享乐。

When he arrived at the mountain pass and

met the granny,

he did not flinch.

He did not take the gold.

小儿子跨上石马，马活了。他骑着马，翻越烈焰熊熊的火山，红红的火焰扑过来，皮肤被火烧着，滋滋地响。

The youngest son mounted the big stone horse.

The horse came alive and took him over the fire mountain.

The flames raged and lashed all around him and his skin sizzled with the intense heat.

越过了火山，他又跳进漂浮着冰块的大海。

海浪夹着大冰块冲击过来，打得身上又冷又痛。

他咬紧牙关，忍着疼痛。终于他到达了大海另一边的太阳山。

Once safely across the fire mountain,

he then ventured out to cross the treacherous ocean. The waves and

icy rocks crashed and thundered about him.

He was bruised and frozen but he did not give up.

He clenched his teeth and fought against the cold and pain. Eventually

he reached the Sun Mountain on the other side of the ocean.

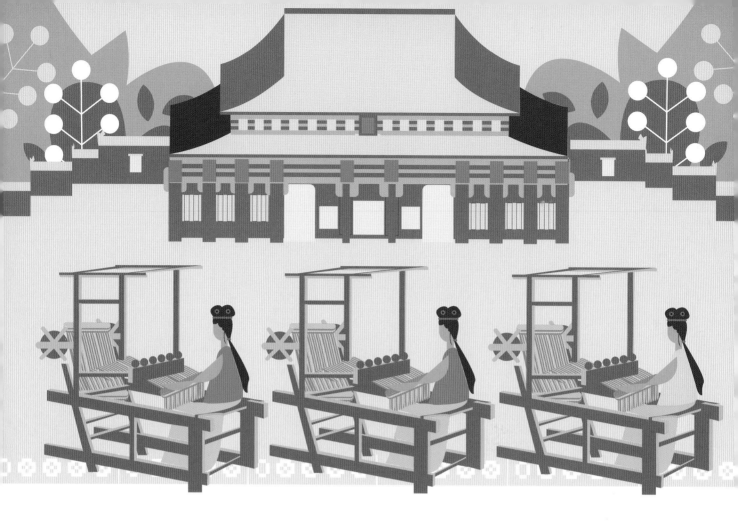

太阳山顶上有一座金碧辉煌的大房子。

小儿子走进大门，看见一群美丽的仙女围在厅堂里织锦。

阿咪的壮锦摆在中间，大家依照它来学织。

On the top of the Sun Mountain stood a magnificent mansion.
He entered the mansion, where he saw a group of pretty fairies
within the hall. His mother's brocade was hung on the wall and
all the fairies were learning to weave by using it as an example.

他向仙女们说明了来意，
她们答应织完后就马上把壮锦还给他。
有一个穿红衣的仙女，因为太喜欢这幅壮锦了，
偷偷在妲布的壮锦上绣上了自己的肖像。

He explained his quest to the fairies.
They promised to return the brocade to him
as soon as they had finished weaving.
A beautiful fairy dressed in red embroidered an image of herself
onto the Zhuang brocade in admiration of his mother's work.

第二天，仙女们把壮锦还给了小儿子。

他收好壮锦，骑上马往家赶。

The next day, the fairies kept their promise and returned
the Zhuang brocade.
The youngest son packed it away carefully and hurried back home.

小儿子回到家时，妈妈已经奄奄一息了。

他赶紧拿出壮锦，那耀眼的光彩使得妈妈的眼睛重见光明，身体也恢复了。

When he arrived home,

he found his mother was on the verge of death.

He unpacked the Zhuang brocade and

its dazzling brilliance magically lit up his mother's eyes

and she was healed instantly.

娘儿俩走到门外，把壮锦展开在地上。一阵香风吹来，他们住的茅草屋不见了，只见眼前是漂亮的房子、美丽的田园，和壮锦上织的一模一样。花园里有个红衣姑娘正在赏花，她正是太阳山的那个红衣仙女。

The Mother and Son went out of the gate and spread the Zhuang brocade onto the ground. There was a sudden fresh breeze and their thatched hut vanished. Instead, there now stood lovely houses and beautiful fields exactly the same as those depicted on the brocade. A lovely girl wearing red robes was smelling the flowers in the garden. She was the fairy he had met on the Sun Mountain.

小儿子和美丽的仙女结了婚，

从此和妈妈一起过着幸福的生活。

Sometime later,

the youngest son married the beautiful fairy.

The lovely couple and their mother lived happily ever after.

大儿子和二儿子花光了老奶奶给的金子，

他们没脸再去见妈妈和弟弟，只得到处乞讨。

The eldest son and the middle son

had spent all the gold given to them.

They were too ashamed to return home.

They had to spent the rest of their days roaming the land

and begging for food.